Hippo isn't Happy

First published in 2008 by
Franklin Watts
338 Euston Road
London
NW1 3BH

Franklin Watts Australia
Level 17/207 Kent Street
Sydney
NSW 2000

A CIP catalogue record for this book is available
from the British Library.

ISBN 978 0 7496 7884 5 (hbk)
ISBN 978 0 7496 7890 6 (pbk)

Series Editor: Jackie Hamley
Series Advisor: Dr Hilary Minns
Series Designer: Peter Scoulding

Printed in China

Franklin Watts is a division of
Hachette Children's Books,
an Hachette Livre UK company.

Hippo isn't Happy

by Marion Rose

Illustrated by Daniel Howarth

W

FRANKLIN WATTS

LONDON•SYDNEY

Marion Rose

"My oh my!

I've written
about a fly!"

**Daniel
Howarth**

"'Luckily for me, my
studio is full of spiders
so the flies tend to keep
away... I just wish
the spiders would
follow them!"

Hippo isn't happy at all.

A buzz-z-z-z she hears
in one of her ears.

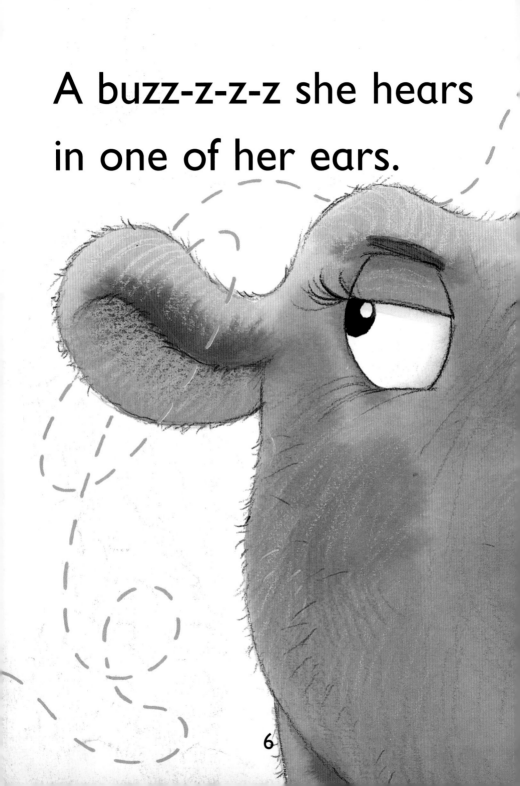

6

She tries to doze ...

... but it's there
on her nose!

It tickles and teases
and sets off ...

... six sneezes!

She runs and wriggles,
and jumps and jiggles.

17

18

SPLAT! With a thud, hippo lands in the mud.

And the fly does a flop
with the hippo on top.

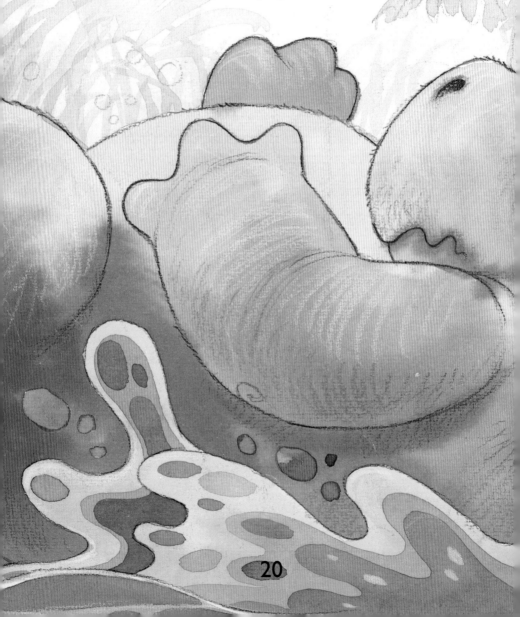

Now that fly isn't happy at all!

Notes for adults

TADPOLES are structured to provide support for newly independent readers. The stories may also be used by adults for sharing with young children.

Starting to read alone can be daunting. **TADPOLES** help by providing visual support and repeating words and phrases. These books will both develop confidence and encourage reading and rereading for pleasure.

If you are reading this book with a child, here are a few suggestions:

1. Make reading fun! Choose a time to read when you and the child are relaxed and have time to share the story.
2. Talk about the story before you start reading. Look at the cover and the blurb. What might the story be about? Why might the child like it?
3. Encourage the child to reread the story, and to retell the story in their own words, using the illustrations to remind them what has happened.
4. Discuss the story and see if the child can relate it to their own experience, or perhaps compare it to another story they know.
5. Give praise! Remember that small mistakes need not always be corrected.

If you enjoyed this book, why not try another TADPOLES story?

Sammy's Secret
978 0 7496 6890 7

Stroppy Poppy
978 0 7496 6893 8

I'm Taller Than You!
978 0 7496 6894 5

Leo's New Pet
978 0 7496 6891 4

Mop Top
978 0 7946 6895 2

Charlie and the Castle
978 0 7496 6896 9

Over the Moon!
978 0 7496 6897 6

Five Teddy Bears
978 0 7496 7292 8

My Sister is a Witch!
978 0 7496 6898 3

Little Troll
978 0 7496 7293 5

The Sad Princess
978 0 7496 7294 2

Runny Honey
978 0 7496 7295 9

Dog Knows Best
978 0 7496 7297 3

Sam's Sunflower
978 0 7496 7298 0

My Big New Bed
978 0 7496 7156 3 (hbk)
978 0 7496 7299 7 (pbk)

My Auntie Susan
978 0 7496 7157 0 (hbk)
978 0 7496 7300 0 (pbk)

Bad Luck, Lucy!
978 0 7496 7158 7 (hbk)
978 0 7496 7302 4 (pbk)

At the End of the Garden
978 0 7496 7159 4 (hbk)
978 0 7496 7303 1 (pbk)

Bertie and the Big Balloon
978 0 7496 7161 7 (hbk)
978 0 7496 7305 5 (pbk)

Pirate Pete
978 0 7496 7160 0 (hbk)
978 0 7496 7304 8 (pbk)